Tammy "Toodlepepper" to the RESCUE

Y0-AGS-169

Written by Tracey Reeder
Illustrated by Brent Putze

The First Rescue

It wasn't until it appeared on the television that we realized nobody knew. Paula and I knew. How come nobody else knew who the mysterious rescuer was? After all, she wasn't that hard to find, but then again, knowing Tammy Toodlepepper, she did have the knack of staying out of the limelight. Some people might think that is normal. But they didn't know Tammy Toodlepepper.

Tammy Toodlepepper had been in the news so much lately. She had carried out all sorts of rescues – nothing was too big or too small for her. She just always seemed to be in the right place at the right time.

Many people were surprised by her heroic actions and the range of skills that she had used, but not us. Nothing Tammy Toodlepepper did ever surprised us.

I remember the day the first rescue happened quite clearly.

This is how the television reported it…

"Good day, viewers. My name is Robin Reward and I am reporting today from the intersection of Eastside Road and Bayberry Street.

"Usually, this is a fairly deserted intersection. Locals have told us that only about ten cars would pass this way each day.

"However, today, the place turned into a shambles when three cars collided.

"Two of the drivers were seriously injured. The third driver received injuries to both legs, but he remained conscious throughout the entire rescue. It is his recollection of the events that we are reporting today.

"Mr. Harding, I'm sorry about the injuries to your legs, but I'm glad to hear that the injuries you sustained are not serious. I'm also pleased that the two other drivers are in hospital in a stable condition and they are both expected to make full recoveries as well. Please share with us the events of this afternoon," said the television reporter.

"Thank you," said Mr. Harding. "Well, from my point of view, it happened fast. I was approaching the intersection and I saw two other vehicles also approaching, so I slowed down. The next thing, the other vehicles collided and one of them veered over and hit me. My car flipped like a toy and my legs were pinned under the steering wheel.

"I wasn't sure how long I lay there like that, but then I heard a big "hi-de-ho" and a woman with a mop of red hair was up on top of the car," the driver explained.

"Did you notice anything else about her?" the reporter asked.

"Well, I don't mean to seem rude, but she sure looked funny! When you are stuck in a flipped car with your legs pinned, you really want help. This woman didn't look like the kind of person that would be any help," the driver continued. "Her clothes were weird! She had on a camouflage-style suit but, instead of being brown and green, hers was pink and orange!"

"Your first impressions were wrong though, weren't they?" the reporter prompted.

"Yeah, they sure were. I really learned a lesson about judging people by the way they look. She sprang into action, talking in a calm tone all the time, asking questions about my family and what I did. She said she had already called the ambulance and that she would just pop away and get something out of her bag. Next thing, she was back and cutting away at the crumpled steering column that had trapped my legs.

"Once she'd done that, I could move my legs, although they were hurting really badly. It was only then that she said she knew she shouldn't move me, but my car was going to blow up and she had to get me out before it did.

"She was so strong, too. She just sort of pulled me out the door and, almost before I had time to yell with pain, I was on the ground, far away enough to be safe. Next to me were the two people from the other vehicles. She had already got them out of their cars and had them in the recovery position. They were covered with what must have been some of her clothes. One was covered with a big yellow waterproof coat with fake fur lining, and the other was draped in something that looked like the pink-and-orange suit she was wearing.

"Just as the cars exploded into a mass of flames

and smoke, the ambulance arrived and she seemed to fade into the background – if you can believe that someone wearing pink and orange can fade into the background. She vanished as quickly as she had arrived and I still have no idea who she is," said the driver.

"She saved your life," the reporter said.

"Oh yeah, mine and the two other drivers'. I wish I knew who she was, and I'm sorry that my first impression was so wrong. Whoever she is, I will be indebted to her for life," the driver finished. "I'd like to be able to thank her in person."

"So there you have it," said Robin Reward as the camera cut from the driver to the reporter, "a mysterious woman in bright camouflage clothing, showing extraordinary skills, saves the lives of three people and then just fades away.

"Perhaps you know this woman. If so, you are lucky. Certainly three people here today are truly lucky that she crossed their paths.

"This is Robin Reward reporting for 1 Z News."

This is what Tammy Toodlepepper had to say about it…

"It was you, wasn't it?" Paula asked Tammy Toodlepepper the next afternoon.

"Me, doing what exactly?" she replied.

"You're the woman that everyone is calling a hero for saving those people from the car accident," Paula continued.

"There was nothing heroic about it. I just happened to be at the right place at the right time. Anyone else would have done the same thing," Tammy replied.

"But most people wouldn't have the sort of equipment in their car that you have," I said.

"You just never know when you might need one

of those cutting things," she replied. "I must admit, it did come in handy."

"Most people wouldn't have risked their own lives in that dangerous situation," said Paula.

"I didn't risk my life. There was plenty of time," Tammy demurred.

That sort of response was Tammy to a T. She was an extremely selfless person who seemed to have acquired all sorts of valuable skills somewhere along the interesting paths she had taken in her life. She was always helping people.

The Second Rescue

"Hello, viewers, I'm Robin Reward and today's Roving Report comes to you from Torbay Beach.

"Well, it seems she has done it again. Our mysterious rescue woman has saved the lives of two youngsters who got caught in a tidal rip just at the mouth of this river.

"This is Willy Brown, the children's grandfather. Tell us what happened, Mr. Brown," said Reward.

"It all happened so fast. The children were playing in the shallow water by the bank of the river. My wife Mary and I were sitting in the shade by that tree. Suddenly, a big wave came up from the beach and completely covered the children. It then receded and took the children with it. We both jumped up, but before we could get to the water, this woman came running over the sand dunes. She threw me her phone and told me to call for help. Next thing I know she's in the water and swimming to the children.

"She looked really funny; she was wearing a kind of old-fashioned swimsuit. You know, the baggy sort with the legs down to the knees. It had purple and green stripes.

"She may have looked funny, but she was a strong swimmer. As soon as I saw her powering through the water, I felt less worried. I knew she would do a better job of saving my grandchildren than I could have done.

"In no time at all, she was floating on her back with her arms safely tucked around the children. Her legs were doing all the work, kicking strongly, almost like a horse.

"Mary was getting very worried as the woman and the children didn't seem to be coming any closer. In fact, they seemed to moving out to sea. But I could see what the woman was doing. She was going with the rip and, as soon as the rip started to weaken, she'd change direction and kick frantically again, out to the side of the rip. Then she'd change direction again, heading back in to the shore from the far end of the beach.

"We rushed to meet her and were helping her get the children out of the water when the rescue squad arrived and took over.

"I saw the woman in the background. She looked a bit like a drowned rat with this big mop of red hair stuck to her face, but we were so worried about the children that we didn't get a chance to thank her before she was gone," said Mr. Brown.

"She saved the children's lives?" asked the reporter, eager for drama.

"Oh, there's no doubt about it. The children can't swim very well. I would have done my best, but I'm not a strong swimmer either. There was no one else on the beach apart from Mary," said Mr. Brown.

"Whoever you are, I would like to thank you from the bottom of my heart. I'm sorry that we didn't take the opportunity to thank you at the time, but things just seemed to happen so quickly," Mr. Brown said right to the camera.

"There you have it, viewers," said Robin Reward, "a mysterious woman in a bright old-fashioned swimsuit with a mop of red hair carries out a heroic act that saves two young children from drowning.

"The description of this woman is very similar to that of the woman who saved three lives after a car accident three days ago.

"Do we have some kind of modern-day superhero living among us? Or is this just an ordinary woman who happens to have been in the right place at the right time?

"Whichever it is, we are certainly lucky to have her around.

"This is Robin Reward, reporting for I Z News."

This is what Tammy Toodlepepper had to say about it…

"Hi, Tammy," I called as I knocked briskly on her front door.

"Come on in," we heard her call from the back of the house.

Paula and I walked down the long hall to the back room where we found Tammy working out on her alpine climber.

"I've only got five more minutes to go," she puffed. "Won't be long."

"I guess you have to keep up your fitness for all the rescuing you're doing," Paula said. "Did you know that you're famous as 'the mysterious rescuer with a mop of red hair?' Robin Reward says you're a modern-day superhero!"

"I don't know what all the fuss is about," Tammy puffed. "I just seem to be in the right place at the right time, that's all. I didn't do anything special. I just saw those children getting into trouble. I also saw their grandparents and decided that I would probably be a better swimmer than both of them, so in I jumped."

"Some people wouldn't risk their lives for people they didn't know," I said.

"Well, that's just silly. I knew I would be all right in that water and the rescue squad were on their way," Tammy said, getting off the alpine climber and starting to do push-ups on the floor. "I'll just do a quick 20 push-ups and some stretches to cool down. Then we can have a drink and some cake," she said with a grin. "All this exercise has given me quite an appetite."

The Third Rescue

"Hello, my name is Robin Reward and I am reporting today from the Midlevels Highway, where it seems our mysterious rescue woman has saved the day yet again.

"Just over an hour ago, we received a call to say that a large cattle truck had overturned and the cows that had escaped were causing havoc all over the highway.

"Thanks largely to the special skills of our mystery rescue woman, there have been no human casualties in this incident. There have also been few cow casualties, though several animals were crushed when the truck overturned.

"Mrs. Ginna, you were in one of the cars at the

scene. Please tell us what happened," the reporter asked earnestly.

"Well, it was really quite frightening. The truck was just ahead of me, so I saw exactly what happened. The truck looked overloaded to me. It veered to one side and then to the other side before it toppled over altogether. There was a loud screeching of brakes as cars darted all over the place to avoid the oncoming truck. It was just lucky that the truck didn't hit or land on any other cars. I slammed on my brakes and then, for some reason, I looked in my rearview mirror. I think I had realized that I wasn't going to hit anything and I wanted to be sure that no one was going to hit me from behind. I was very lucky – a few other cars banged into each other trying to get out of the way. But it didn't look too serious.

"Next thing I knew, there were cows all over the highway. They were running around in panic and kicking out at cars. Some really stupid people were honking their horns, which just made the poor things more distressed.

"But I must have been a little hysterical, because I'm afraid I started laughing – it was such a spectacle! And suddenly this very odd woman appeared. Boy, she made me laugh even more.

"She had this great mop of red hair springing out from beneath a green hat. Her dress had pink and brown stripes, and I think she was wearing big white boots. Her arms were full of hay.

"Even though it was a serious situation, I laughed and laughed because she was calling 'Here cowsie, cowsie, come here' as she made a trail of hay leading off to the side of the highway.

"My first thought was, what on Earth is this silly woman doing? But as I watched, I realized that she wasn't as silly as I thought; the cows were beginning to take notice of her and head for the hay. Other people caught on to what she was doing and came up slowly behind the cows to help herd them in the right direction," Mrs. Ginna said.

"Do you think that this woman saved people's or cows' lives?" the reporter asked.

"Of course she did. Once I pulled myself together I suddenly realized that she had almost single-handedly saved the cows and probably many more car accidents as the cows rushed into the oncoming traffic," Mrs. Ginna responded.

"So what happened to her?" the reporter asked. "Where did she go?"

"Well, that's the strange thing. You would think that in all those loud clothes it would be hard for anyone to slip away quietly, but that's exactly what she did. I watched her walk back to her car and get another bale of hay out of the trunk, which she swung onto her back and took over to the cows that had settled on the side of the highway, munching very contentedly.

"A few of the others and I began helping distribute the hay, and when I looked around, the car and the woman were gone," Mrs. Ginna said.

"Did you happen to get a close look at the car?" asked the reporter.

"Only to see that it was a pink sports car," Mrs. Ginna replied.

"Well, there you have it, viewers. Our mysterious rescue woman helps out again, and this time we have another piece of the puzzle. Not only does she have her own distinctive style of dressing, but she drives a pink sports car. Is this anyone you know? We'd sure like to get in contact with her to thank her in person," the reporter said.

"This is Robin Reward reporting for 1 Z News."

This is what Tammy Toodlepepper had to say about it...

"Hi," called Tammy, jumping the gate as usual and bounding up our garden path.

"There is no end to your list of talents," our dad said, smiling at her.

"I've learned a lot of skills from a lot of people

over time, and every now and again they come in handy," Tammy said, smiling back.

"How did you manage to have all that hay in your car?" I asked her curiously.

"Pea straw, actually," Tammy replied. "Cows like to eat pea straw."

"What was pea straw doing in your car then?" Paula asked.

Tammy smiled. "It's for my vegetable garden, of course. Well, it was going to be, anyway. Now I'll have to go back to the farm and get some more. Still, the cows might have ended up with the pea straw, but I ended up with something even better for the garden."

"Don't tell me," Dad said, "cow manure."

"How'd you know?" Tammy asked, surprised.

"Oh, it says at the end of this article that some motorists thought they had seen you later that night with a shovel and sack clearing up after the cows," Dad said, holding up the newspaper.

"I got two sacks full," Tammy said. "That will make the beans and carrots grow nicely."

We all laughed.

The Fourth Rescue

"Hello, viewers, my name is Robin Reward and I am reporting today from the Ridgeview National Park, where our mysterious rescue woman has been at work again. It seems she happened to stumble upon a hiker whose friend had fallen down a cliff.

"Peter Packer and his friend Dina Wells had come up into the National Park for a day of hiking. They'd been walking for about an hour when Peter lost his footing in the shingle and slid off the side of this cliff. He didn't fall too far, but he landed awkwardly and looked like he was in a lot of pain.

"Dina, we're glad that Peter is okay and pleased that you could return with us to this spot to share with us the events surrounding this morning's daring rescue," said the Robin Reward.

"Thank you. First I'd like to take this opportunity to thank the woman who saved Peter's life. Her brave, unselfish act means that Peter is safe and recuperating in the hospital," Dina said.

"Tell us what went through your head when you first caught a glimpse of the woman walking up the track," the reporter urged.

"I was so pleased to see someone that I didn't take much notice of who she was or what she was wearing. It was not until a bit later that I began to think that she didn't look like she would be much help," Dina said.

"But you were very wrong, weren't you?" asked Robin Reward.

"Thankfully, I was. She bounded up to me and when she realized what I was trying to tell her in my hysterical state, she sprang into action, reassuring me that everything would be all right.

"She assessed the situation and decided that the best thing to do would be to rappel down the cliff to where Peter was lying. She swung her pack off her back and pulled out all this specialized equipment. Then she threw a phone to me and asked me to call for help. She also told me the location to tell them, which was a relief because I didn't have a clue where in the National Park we were. It wasn't until I put the phone down that her clothing drew my attention. It was normal hiking gear – sweat top and pants with hiking boots and a jacket. It was just the colors that made them seem odd; they were kind of rainbow patterned. Her boots were orange with a green trim. Her hair

was a wild mass of red curls.

"She used that large tree over there as a base for all the ropes she needed and showed me how to help lower her down. To be honest, I was terrified, but she seemed to know what she was doing and, until the rescue squad arrived, there was only us to help Peter.

"She grabbed a smaller pack out of her large pack and over the side she went.

"When she got down to Peter, she gave me a big thumbs up. I felt relieved as I watched her work. She didn't move Peter, just wrapped a blanket she got from her pack around him. Peter's right arm seemed to be bleeding rather badly, so she pressed a folded-up towel, which she also produced from her pack, firmly onto the wound until the bleeding began to lessen.

"Another big thumbs-up sign, and then we just had to wait. It seemed like hours to me, but it was actually only 30 minutes before we heard the noise of the helicopter that the rescue squad sent to rescue Peter. When it arrived, it winched down a paramedic who soon had Peter winched up on a kind of stretcher. At that stage I and the mystery lady made our way down the mountain to where the helicopter would land outside the lodge. I was so relieved to see Peter safe, if battered and bruised, that I completely forgot to look out for the woman who had been so helpful.

"When I asked the rescue squad team about her, they were full of praise for her. According to them, without her help Peter would have been in much worse shape.

"After we had come back to the lodge, no one saw where she went from there," Dina said.

"You and Peter are grateful to her, then?" the reporter asked.

"Gosh, that's an understatement. I only wish that I had made more of an effort to thank her in person. But if you are watching, thank you ever so much for your help today," Dina said, as she turned to the camera.

"A woman like this could not be just another face in the crowd," said the reporter directly to the camera. "She must have good friends out there who know who she is, but who know that for one reason or another she does not wish to be identified. So from all of us here at 1 Z and all of those people you have helped, thank you," the reporter continued.

"This is Robin Reward, reporting for 1 Z News."

This is what Tammy Toodlepepper had to say about it…

"Hello," I called to Tammy as we rounded the corner of the house.

"Hi," Tammy called from the hot tub she had built herself. "I'm out here in the tub. I've had a long hard week so I thought I would give the old body a bit of a treat and soak in here for a while," she said.

"You sure have been busy. Those hikers were very lucky you came along when you did," Paula said.

"I just happened to be in the right place at the right time," Tammy replied. "No big deal."

"You seem to have been in the right place at the right time a lot lately," I chuckled.

"Yeah," said Tammy. "Isn't it lucky? I do like to be able to help people."

The Fifth Rescue

"Good day, viewers, this is Robin Reward with today's Roving Report. I'm standing on the corner of Smith and Turtle Streets, where I'm speaking to Lily Collins and her cat, Sooty.

"Lily, can you tell us what happened to her?" asked Robin Reward.

Lily sniffed. "Well, my cat – she's still a kitten, really – was sitting just outside my gate sunning herself, when two boys and a dog came along. The dog was on a leash, so I didn't expect anything to happen. But when they saw poor Sooty, the boys let the dog leap at her!

"Poor Sooty ran for her life, the dog racing after her in full cry, while those horrible boys just stood there and laughed. Luckily, she raced up a tree, where she was safe enough from the dog, who was circling the foot of the tree and growling. I asked the boys to put their dog back on the leash, but they laughed at me, too.

"I was so upset, I didn't know what to do next. And then along came someone I was very glad to see – a woman with a mop of curly red hair. She was dressed in an assortment of crazy gear so bright it made your eyes ache to look at her. She asked what was happening, and I explained as well as I could through my tears.

"She fixed the dog with a steely glare and told it to sit. It sat. Next, she told the two boys to put their dog back on the leash and that they should be ashamed of themselves. Believe it or not, they did as they were told and they slunk away shamefaced!

"The woman turned to me then and asked me if I had a ladder handy. I didn't, but she said it didn't matter and took a coiled rope out of her big bag, which she threw up and over a sturdy branch, knotting it securely. Then she climbed that rope like a monkey, right up to the branch where Sooty crouched. She put Sooty in her bag, attached the rope to the bag, and lowered her down to me first. Then she coiled up the rope and slid down the trunk."

"Do you know who Sooty's rescuer is?" asked Robin Reward.

"Oh yes," said Lily. "I know her well. I'd love to tell you her name, but I'm afraid I promised her I wouldn't. She doesn't want any attention from the media. But I can tell you that she's a friend of everybody in this part of the world. She's always helping people."

"Well, thank you for your story," said Robin Reward, who sounded very disappointed that the identity of the mystery woman was still a mystery. After all, he was a reporter, and it was his job to find out things. However, luck was about to be on his side.

This is what Tammy Toodlepepper had to say about it…

Paula and I were sitting around Tammy's kitchen table drinking lemonade.

"Lily told me how grateful she was to you for saving Sooty," I said as I sipped.

"Oh, it was nothing to make a fuss about," said Tammy. "The dog was no problem, it was just doing what dogs generally do if there's a cat around."

The Rescued Reporter

"Good day, viewers, my name is Robin Reward and I'm reporting today from the Bluegull Hospital, where I'll be a guest for a few days after breaking a leg when I fell from my bicycle.

"I was lucky enough to fall from my bike when the front wheel hit a stone as I cycled quickly down a quiet country lane.

"What is lucky about that, you may well ask? The lucky part is that the first person to help me as I lay in a crumpled heap in the road was driving a pink sports car.

"As the car rolled to a stop, the first thing I saw was a woman with a large mop of red curly hair. It was pulled back off her face by a blue scarf.

"The next thing I saw was a green dress covered in yellow spots, lacy stockings, and sports shoes.

"'It's her,' I thought, 'it's really her!' And, just as the people I interviewed described, she took charge of the situation with great skill. In no time at all, she had covered my grazes with antiseptic and gauze, and splinted my leg with a couple of sticks she found along the side of the road.

"Then, with me safely tucked up in a blanket in the passenger seat, she tied the bent remains of my bicycle onto the top of the car and we were off to the nearest emergency room.

"I asked her many questions about herself and her life, including where she had learned her numerous skills. She said she had watched, learned, and taken advice from the many extraordinary people she had met throughout her life.

"To all this, she said, she has added her own personal style.

"This exceptional woman has asked us not to broadcast her name, but nevertheless there are many things we can all learn from such a person and the example she sets. I am glad that I was lucky enough to have crossed her path.

"This is Robin Reward, reporting for 1 Z News."

A Thank-You Party Planned

When Paula and I had watched Robin Reward's latest report, we started talking.

"I know Tammy doesn't want any fuss to be made about her rescue efforts," I said, "but it seems wrong not to do something to recognize all the things she does for people."

"Mmmm," said Paula, and I could practically see her mind working. "What would Tammy appreciate most from her friends? Something she would like… what about a party?"

"A party! That would be terrific!" I said enthusiastically. "We could invite all the people that Tammy has rescued. We'd have to find out where they lived," I added as an afterthought.

But Paula had another brainwave.

"I know. Let's ask Robin Reward to host the party!" she exclaimed.

"You heard him on TV today, he's really grateful to Tammy. He'd be able to get all the rescued people to come, too."

So we went and talked to Dad about the idea.

Dad was as enthusiastic as we were and promised to help us in whatever way he could. So, I phoned the Bluegull Hospital and asked to speak to Mr. Reward. The person I spoke to didn't want to put me through to him at first, saying he was resting. But I persisted and eventually I got through.

As I explained the party idea, Paula stood beside me straining to try and catch what Robin Reward was saying on the other end of the phone. I smiled at her reassuringly as I listened, to let her know that he liked the idea. By the time I hung up, I had a promise from Robin Reward that he would hold a surprise party for the mysterious rescue woman. All Paula and I had to do was make sure that Tammy turned up in the right place at the right time.

That was easier said than done, actually. A few days after the call, we received an invitation in the post. It was marked "secret" and it was from Robin Reward. The party was to be held in a week's time at the I Z TV studios.

"I guess that will give Mr. Reward plenty of time to learn to walk on his crutches," said Paula.

"Well," I said, "that's his problem. Ours is getting Tammy to the party. How are we going to do it?"

"I think I can probably help you there," said Dad.

"I'll ask Tammy to take you two for a tour of the I Z TV studios. She won't realize there's a party until she's inside."

The Party

It all worked out brilliantly. Tammy was happy to take Paula and me for a tour of the studios. On a sunny day one week later, the three of us were zooming along in her pink sports car on our way to the I Z TV studios. I felt a little anxious, just in case Tammy was not pleased to have a surprise party sprung on her, after she'd said that she didn't want anyone to make a fuss. Yet, here we were, making a fuss. I reassured myself by remembering that she was a person who had always *liked* surprises.

We arrived at the studio gates, where the security guard smiled and waved us through. Tammy parked the car and we all jumped out.

"Now, which way first?" asked Tammy. "Where

does the tour start from?"

Paula and I looked at each other. "Let's go into the lobby and ask at reception," I said.

"Lead on, then," said Tammy, and we marched inside the large glass doors of the biggest building. Inside, the first thing we saw was an arrow sign, pointing down a hall.

"It must be this way," said Tammy. "How exciting! I've been to a lot of places but I've never visited a television studio before."

"Look, another arrow!" exclaimed Paula. "We must turn left here."

We turned left and were faced with another arrow, pointing up.

"We must be supposed to take the elevator," I said. "What floor should we go to?"

"The top, of course!" said Paula, firmly.

"Do you think we'll get to meet any stars?" I asked. "Although it's weird, the whole building seems to be empty. I hope there hasn't been a fire alarm!"

At that point the elevator doors opened.

"Surprise!" shouted the voices of all the people who filled the big room in front of us. Even I got a surprise, and I'd been expecting one! As for Tammy, for the first time ever since we'd got to

know her when our family moved into her street,
she was speechless.

Then Robin Reward hopped over on his

crutches. "Welcome to your party, Tammy Toodlepepper! This is to say thank you for all those wonderful rescues you've made. We're all very grateful."

And there was Mr. Harding, who Tammy had

dragged from his car just before it exploded, and the Browns with their grandchildren, who Tammy had saved from drowning.

There was Mrs. Ginna and the cattle-truck driver and Peter Packer and Dina Wells. There was Lily Collins (without her cat), and our parents, and a lot of people from where we live. There were balloons and music and a mountain of food.

I ran and got Tammy a cold drink, because she was so surrounded by people who wanted to thank her in person that I knew she would be there for a while. I handed it to her, then Paula and I went and helped ourselves to platefuls of yummy party food. We thought we deserved it after our efforts, and while we sat and ate, we played at spotting the TV stars in the crowd. There seemed to be quite a number of them.

At last the crowd around Tammy thinned. Tammy caught my eye and Paula and I went over, carrying our plates.

"I want a word with you two," Tammy began in a stern voice. But it was no good; she was having a hard time keeping the smile from her face. "I said I didn't want any fuss!"

"Sorry, Tammy," said Paula, "you just have to accept the fact that we think you're a special person who should be made a fuss of now and then."

"Well, I am having a fantastic time," Tammy admitted. "It's so nice to meet all these people again under happier circumstances."

I tried to reply, but I didn't. I couldn't speak. I had breathed in a peanut and I was choking. I gasped, but no air came into my lungs. I gasped again. I was really panicking now.

Tammy Toodlepepper swung into action. Calmly, she moved behind me and put her arms around my middle and squeezed hard. I coughed, and the peanut flew out of my mouth. I dropped to my knees, wheezing as I gulped in air.

"You'll be okay," said Tammy beside me. "Take calm, deep breaths. Steady now."

My parents had rushed over when they heard the commotion, and Paula was hovering anxiously; they all had looks of relief on their faces as they saw I was all right. Dad spoke first.

"Well, I guess a party to thank the mysterious rescue woman wouldn't be complete without a real rescue!" he said. "Thank you, Tammy."

"You're welcome," she smiled "I learned the Heimlich maneuver in a first-aid course I took. It's been very useful on more than one occasion."

I croaked, "Thanks, Tammy. And, guess what? I've decided to do a first-aid course, so I can be prepared in case of emergencies, too."

"That's an excellent idea," said Tammy Toodlepepper enthusiastically. "You just never know when you're going to come across a person who needs rescuing."